CALICO ILLUSTRATED CLASSICS

Mary Shelley's

Frankenstein

ADAPTED BY: Dottie Enderle
ILLUSTRATED BY: Eric Scott Fisher

magic
wagon

visit us at www.abdopublishing.com

Published by Magic Wagon, a division of the ABDO Group,
8000 West 78th Street, Edina, Minnesota 55439. Copyright
© 2010 by Abdo Consulting Group, Inc. International copyrights
reserved in all countries. All rights reserved. No part of this book
may be reproduced in any form without written permission from
the publisher.

Calico Chapter Books™ is a trademark and logo of Magic Wagon.

Printed in the United States of America, Melrose Park, Illinois.
102009
012010

 PRINTED ON RECYCLED PAPER

Original text by Mary Shelley
Adapted by Dotti Enderle
Illustrated by Eric Scott Fisher
Edited by Stephanie Hedlund and Rochelle Baltzer
Cover and interior design by Abbey Fitzgerald

Library of Congress Cataloging-in-Publication Data

Enderle, Dotti, 1954-
  Frankenstein / adapted by Dotti Enderle ; illustrated by Eric Scott
Fisher ; based upon the works of Mary Shelley.
      p. cm. -- (Calico illustrated classics)
    ISBN 978-1-60270-705-4 8-24-16
  [1. Monsters--Fiction. 2. Horror stories.] I. Fisher, Eric Scott, ill. II.
Shelley, Mary Wollstonecraft, 1797-1851. Frankenstein. III. Title.
  PZ7.E69645Fr 2010
  [Fic]--dc22
                                        2009036978

Table of Contents

The Icy North

I stand on the deck, looking out. The white snow and ice crystals are blinding. Our ship is stuck as we're trapped here in a glacier.

It is my own fault. It was I who wanted this journey. I craved so badly to see land that very few men have seen. So we sailed north.

The air grew colder, but I continued on. The icebergs we passed grew wider and taller, like small castles peeking out of the ocean. But we sailed through, ignoring the danger.

Several of the crewmen wanted to turn back. "We must return to England while we can," they begged. But I refused to listen. I needed to see more. And now, because of me, the ship is wedged in ice. We can go no farther.

As I stand here, the freezing arctic wind burns my face. I've never been so cold. And not just from the chilly air, but also from fear. Will we die up here?

One of my crewmen approaches. "Captain Walton, please," he said. "What shall we do?"

I hang my head, not knowing what to tell him. They look to me for answers, but I have none. Then I hear a yell, "Come quickly!"

We move toward the voice. "Look!" A crewman points over the side of the ship. "What is that?" he asks.

I lean over the railing to see. There is a bundle of wet fur lying on a large nugget of ice. I see broken pieces of a dogsled beside it. But underneath all that fur, I make out the shape of a man.

"Hurry!" I shout. "Bring him up!"

Several men climb down to rescue this odd stranger. And with great care, we lay him down on a cot below, where it is warm.

The man's face is pale and blue. His breathing is shallow.

"Quick," I say. "Bring blankets." We bundle him up tightly, hoping the warmth will save his life.

After some color returns to his skin, I say, "I am Captain Walton. This is my ship." The man barely moves. He opens his eyes a little. "You are safe now," I reassure him.

But he shakes his head. "No. There is no place safe. Not while he is loose. I mustn't stay here. I have to look for him."

"Who?" I ask. But the man closes his eyes and falls into a deep sleep.

The man is unconscious for several days. His fever is high, and I try to comfort him with cool water. I force him to drink warm tea. Despite my efforts, he only wakes occasionally.

"Must find him!" he shouts. "Must destroy him!" I think it is just the fever causing bad dreams. But finally the man wakes. He carefully pulls himself up.

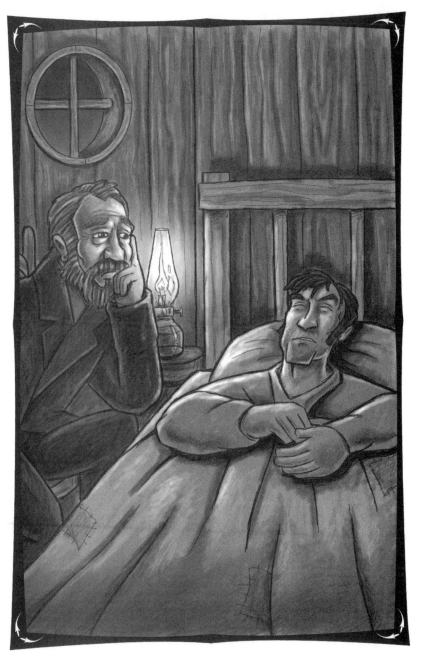

"Let me bring you some soup," I tell him. But he shakes his head.

"You need to eat," I urge. "You need your strength."

The man reaches up, pulling me near. "There is no time," he says. "I must find him."

For days now the man has rambled about finding someone. I asked, "Who must you find?"

"Him," he answers. "The one I created. The monster."

"Tell me," I say. "Who are you? How did you come to be here?"

He takes a deep, raspy breath. His eyes are wild and restless. "I am the man who created a devil. And I followed him here so I can destroy him."

"Please, tell me more," I say. And he does.

Frankenstein's Story

My name is Victor Frankenstein. I come from the city of Geneva. My father was a well-respected man there. He had many friends. But because he worked hard for many years, he didn't marry until he was much older.

He married the daughter of one of his dear friends. Her name was Caroline. It wasn't long until I was born. A few years later, she gave birth to my brother Ernest.

My mother was a kind woman. And because of her kindness, she took in a young girl to live with us. The girl was a peasant named Elizabeth. My mother and father bought her nice clothes and gave her a lovely room to sleep in. Soon, she was like a daughter to them.

Several years after that, my brother William was born. He was small, sweet, and wonderful. We were a happy family.

I went to school and studied hard. I loved learning, especially math and science. I spent more time with my book than with my friends.

Then I met Henry Clerval, a boy much like me. We enjoyed all the same things. We loved to explore. We loved nature and science. Soon, we became best friends.

I especially liked reading. I spent many, many hours reading to Elizabeth. Even though we grew up in the same house, I never looked at her as my sister. I cared for her, and she cared for me. I always knew that when we grew up we would marry.

One night, a sudden storm blew in. The rain pounded the roof. Thunder boomed like a cannon. And lightning streaked across the sky like broken glass. I found it utterly fascinating. I decided then to devote myself to science and the study of electricity. Everything seemed perfect.

My happiness did not last long. As I was about to leave for the university, my mother died. I stayed, filled with sadness. Her death made me think about life. *Why does someone have to die? Could it be about nature and chemistry?*

I could not grieve forever and knew I must go on. I had to continue my education. So I left my father, Elizabeth, Ernest, William, and Henry and journeyed on to the university.

I studied all of the time with little rest. I especially loved chemistry. I loved how everything we do and see and feel was a part of a chemical makeup. It fascinated me.

So I continued to study and study and study, and soon I formulated an idea. I had no way of knowing that the idea would eventually destroy my life.

The Creation

I made a laboratory on the second floor of my apartment. It was large and empty, and I knew I would not be disturbed there. I kept the lab locked so it would remain a secret.

I spent hours studying the human body. I learned about everything from the blinking of eyes to the twitch of the smallest toe. I was fascinated by what lay within a person's flesh.

Soon my laboratory was filled with notes and books. The tables were lined with jars and beakers. Even in the day I burned candles for light because I kept the windows shut tight. I could not risk anyone seeing my project.

Hours turned into days. Days turned into months. Sometimes I forgot to eat. I'd make

myself stop long enough to swallow a f
of bread. I never quit working.

Without proper nourishment, I began to resemble the skeletons that dangled inside my lab. I had lost far too much weight.

When I did look in the mirror, it seemed as though a stranger was staring back. My cheeks had become hollow. My eyes appeared red and tired. And my greasy hair grew wild around my face.

But I kept going.

I only left my lab when necessary, and usually at night. I would sneak into cemeteries searching for fresh graves. I never brought a lantern. I couldn't take a chance on being seen.

What I was doing was an unspeakable crime, but I had no other choice. Where else would I get the parts I so badly needed?

So I worked only by moonlight when I could. Some nights the darkness made it difficult to work. I would trip over broken branches or stones that were left to mark a grave. But I didn't mind the scratches and bruises. I was there for a reason, and nothing would stop me.

The shadows would stretch gray and thin as I walked through the cemeteries, searching for newly dug graves. I could always tell when it was fresh. The dirt on the most recent graves was black and piled high. And most were surrounded by fresh flowers.

That's when I'd dig. Sometimes I would hear the distant bark of a dog or the call of an owl. I would freeze in fear, wondering if I'd been caught.

I would dig and dig and dig, throwing the dirt aimlessly over my shoulder. Then my shovel would hit something hard. I would drop to my knees, scooping the dirt with my hands until I could get to the coffin.

And that's when I'd fill a cloth bag with the things I need. I took bones, veins, brains, and hearts. I kept them stored safely in my lab. At

times I felt the jar full of eyes was staring at me. They waited to see which pair I'd use.

I continued to work on and on. I rarely knew if it was winter or summer. All I cared about was my work. I mapped everything out on a large sheet of paper, for I would not start my creation until everything was perfect.

I sometimes got letters from my family. My father would ask about my studies. Elizabeth would say she missed me. Henry would wonder if I was ever going to return. They worried about me. But I couldn't take the time to reply. I only thought of one thing: my work.

Once I had everything figured out, I began putting the pieces together. I knew my creation had to be large for my plan to work. It must be at least eight feet high.

I sewed the large feet to long, thick legs. The hands were the size of egg baskets. And the head was huge. Sometimes pieces would fall on the floor, but I'd just find fresh ones. I could not stop now.

Bit by bit, it began to form. I stitched and sewed. As it was nearly done, I worried. What if it failed? Had I wasted all this time for nothing?

I wanted to finish, but I couldn't bring life to it without electricity. And to gain that, I would have to wait for a thunderstorm. Until then, I spent hours pouring over my notes.

And then, on a dreary November night, it happened. A raging storm blew into the city. I could hear shutters slamming in the wind. Rain pounded like the devil. I knew I had to hurry.

I placed the brain into its head. Then I sewed in its heart. I wired the creature to a lightning rod that I had put high upon the roof. Thunder shook the room. Lightning lit the sky. Then *pow*! It hit the rod like a whip.

Sparks and fire raced through it. And my creature bounced and shook from the jolt. Then just as quickly, it stopped.

I rushed over, anxious to see. Smoke rose from the body. I could feel the heat before I even touched it. Then I laid my head down on its chest. I listened.

At first I heard nothing. Then, it was there. *Thu-thump . . . thu-thump . . . thu-thump.*

Yes! I had done it! Its heart beat with a healthy rhythm. I ran my hand up his twitching arm. But then, it opened its eyes. It looked right at me. I had succeeded. My creature was alive!

CHAPTER 4

The Creature

I had done it! I had created a man! I would be his master, teaching him as though he were a child. He would learn the beauty of the world. He would see vast oceans and lonely deserts. He would learn math and science, and work alongside me. It was all so perfect.

But then he turned his head and looked at me. His eyes were dull and yellow. His skin looked as sickly green as mold. He opened his mouth and moaned, though it sounded more like a howl. I backed away, frightened. His lip snarled as he sat up.

I moved back, one small step at a time. What had I done? This was not a man. This was a monster!

The creature growled again, sounding like a wolf ready to attack. What should I do?

It stood, towering over me. It was enormous.

I felt myself grow weak. My mind whirled. How could I have done this? I used the proper size hands and feet. I took care to give him everything a healthy human should possess. Why was his brain not working as it should?

He moaned like an animal caught in a trap. But he was not the one trapped. I was. He moved closer and closer and closer.

The storm continued to roar. At times I couldn't tell if I was hearing thunder or the loud bang of his footsteps. He drew even nearer.

I locked the laboratory door, and then I rushed to my room to hide. I curled up in the corner, weeping. *What should I do? How should I handle this? Was he up there, waiting for me?* But the strain of my work caught up with me, and I felt completely drained. Soon I lay down on my bed and fell into a restless sleep.

But there was no peace. I was consumed with horrible nightmares. I dreamed I saw Elizabeth. She smiled and waved, then ran to me. I took her in my arms, holding her tight. But then she changed. Instead of Elizabeth, I was hugging my dead, rotting mother.

I tossed and turned. Even in my sleep I could hear him. I could feel him. His breathing crackled like burning wood.

I startled awake, and there he stood next to my bed, looking down at me. His nostrils flared with each breath. His watery eyes were the color of straw. Every stitch in his face ran with oozing pus. I couldn't bear it.

I had no choice but to flee. And that's what I did. Like a coward, I ran out into the night. The rain stung my face as it beat down on me. I was soon drenched. The cold air gave me shivers. I had no coat or heavy boots. I had nothing but fear.

I stood outside, trembling. Where could I go? Where should I run? I had no time to think. I had to move quickly. The creature would be right behind me.

So I ran. I ran as far away as I could. I imagined seeing him around every corner. Every shadow made me jump. My heart beat wildly. But I had to take shelter.

I crawled inside a doorway, hugging my knees. And again I cried. Two years I had worked. Two years I had slaved. And what had I created? A beast.

I stayed there throughout the night. I thought about my family. How could I have put my work first? I missed my father. I missed Elizabeth. Would I ever see them again?

The rain finally stopped, and the morning sun shone brightly through the clouds. I knew I couldn't stay here any longer. I had to go back. I had to face the monster I had created.

People were coming out of their houses as I walked along. They stared at me. I must have looked horrendous. My damp clothes were clinging to me. My hair was plastered to my face. I was in no hurry. I needed time to think.

As I arrived at my apartment, I stood outside. Should I go in? Is it still lurking inside? I took a step forward, and then I stopped.

"You have to deal with this!" I told myself. But how? Should I trap him? Should I tie him up? Or should I kill him?

I took a deep breath, urging myself to go in. That's when I heard, "Victor!" I jumped.

"Victor! It's me."

I turned to see my old friend, Henry Clerval, crossing the street.

"My goodness, Victor," he said. "You look terrible!"

"Yes," I told him. "I got caught in the rain."

He smiled at me and patted my back.

"Why did you come?" I asked.

"Your father was worried. He sent me."

"I should have written," I said. "I'm sorry."

"Don't be sorry, Victor. I'm just glad you are well."

If Henry had known the truth, he would know I was not well. My body was weak. My mind reeled with confusion. And my heart ached because of what I had done.

"Why haven't we heard from you?" he asked.

"I was working," I replied. Should I tell him the truth?

Henry nodded. "Yes. You always were a hard worker. Now, are you going to invite me in, or will we stay out here all day?"

I looked at the door, wondering if it was safe. What would I tell Henry about the monster? Would I be putting him in danger?

Henry led the way. I was too weak to argue. But I moved ahead of him. "Set your things here in the hall," I said. "I'll be right back."

I checked every inch of the apartment. First I peered into my bedroom. There was nothing there. I crept upstairs to the laboratory. It was empty too. Then I laughed out loud like a crazed fool. Gone. It was gone.

"Come in, Henry!" I called to him.

Henry picked up his bags and stepped inside. I walked toward him, feeling relief. But the night had been too much for me. My body had grown too weak. And standing there, before my best friend, everything went black. I passed out at his feet.

Fever and Failure

Henry put me in my bed, and stayed to look after me. I barely remember a thing. A raging fever overcame me.

Some nights I'd wake up to see Henry by my bed. He forced me to drink soup and tea. But I had no strength at all. Those months of creating the monster had drained me.

Days passed. I spent every moment in bed. Henry read to me, but I only caught a sentence or two. I could not stay awake for more than a few minutes.

My sleep was restless, filled with horrific dreams. I dreamed about my family. I had long, agonizing dreams about Elizabeth. When I reached for her, she'd vanish.

But mostly, I dreamed about the creature. I could still see him standing by me, his lips curled as though he might bite me. I dreamed of his limp and his waxy skin. In my nightmares, he'd grab me and shake me. Then, he'd speak my name, "Victor. Victor."

"Victor!" It was not the monster shaking me, it was Henry. "Wake up, Victor!"

I opened my eyes. Henry stood above me. He looked like he'd seen a ghost.

"Is he here?" I shouted.

"Calm down," Henry said. "You were having a nightmare."

"It's real, Henry! It's real!"

Henry patted my arm. "No, Victor. It was only a dream."

Oh, how I wished it were only a dream. I wanted to tell Henry, but I didn't have the strength.

Henry smiled. "Victor, you were shouting so loudly I thought the walls might fall in."

"It was not a dream," I said.

"It was a dream," Henry argued. "You were shouting about graveyards, and sewing together body pieces, and monsters. Those things are not real. They are only in books or nightmares."

I closed my eyes again. My body still burned with the fever. I could not get up. I had no other choice but to fall back asleep.

When my fever finally broke, I sat up, covered in sweat.

"Welcome back," Henry said. "I thought I might lose you for good."

I looked out the window. I couldn't believe it. I remembered the cold November night. But now, the sun shone in through the window. The air smelled fresh with the fragrance of flowers. Birds sang. It had to be spring.

"You were sick for months," Henry said.

"And you stayed here the whole time?" Henry was truly a great friend. Who else would sit by my side and take care of me for so long? No one else except Elizabeth or my father would take on such a burden. Suddenly I felt homesick. I missed my family.

But I also wondered about the monster. Where was he? Had he survived? Would he come back to destroy me? I hated myself for what I had done and how I'd failed.

Henry brought me more tea. "Now that you are better, I thought I should give you this." He handed me a letter from Elizabeth. For the first time in months my heart felt light.

"I'll leave you alone to read it." He left my room and I heard the front door open and close. I was alone again. Truly alone. I opened the letter and read:

Dear Victor,

I have gotten many letters from Henry. He said that you were ill. Your father and I have worried so much. He wanted to come there, but I knew that Henry would take good care of you.

Do not worry about us. Everyone is fine. Ernest sends his regards. Your father is healthy and busy. And your brother, William, is the same. He's always happy. He loves flying his kite and horseback riding. He keeps the rest of us feeling young.

And you remember our housekeeper, Justine? She has returned. She takes care of all of us and has become a good friend. We are like sisters. William loves her, too. She's so good to him.

Victor, I can't tell you how much I miss you. I think of you every day. Please write to me so I'll know that you are better.

Love, Elizabeth

I held the letter to my heart. Oh, my sweet Elizabeth! How could I have been so cruel? I had turned my back on those who loved me the most.

I managed to get to my desk. I grabbed my pen and ink and wrote her a letter, saying that when I felt stronger, I would return home. I sealed the letter. I would have Henry send it for me.

I was not concerned for myself because I knew Henry would stay with me. And there was no need to worry about my family. They were fine. My only fear now was the monster. As time passed, I assumed he must be dead.

Henry and I spent our days reading, playing chess, and talking science. It took two full weeks before I could walk properly again. But Henry insisted that I not rush. I needed the summer to recover. I wrote a letter to my father, telling him I'd be home in the fall.

I spent that summer introducing Henry to my friends from the university. He began classes there, and I occupied myself by helping him study.

The next spring when the roads were clear, I made plans to return home. It had been a year since my nightmare, and I thought it was all behind me. But then another letter came. This one was from my father.

Dear Victor,

Please return home immediately. Your brother, William, is dead. It was murder.

CHAPTER 6

Murder!

I dropped the letter and fell to the floor, crying, "William!" My dear, sweet brother! Who would do such a thing? Father's heart must be broken. I couldn't waste another moment. I must get back home!

Henry agreed to stay at my apartment because he needed to continue his classes. So I packed my things and gathered my notes and papers. Then I said good-bye.

"Thank you," I told him. "You have been a great friend, and I could never repay you. I would not be here if it weren't for you. I would have wasted away all alone. I will miss you so much."

"And I will miss you as well. Go," Henry urged. "You have not seen your family in six years. Give them my love."

Had it been that long? The years are like a flash before my eyes. I stepped into the carriage and waved good-bye. Soon we were off.

It was a three-day journey to Geneva. But the bumpy carriage took me closer and closer. The countryside was beautiful. The large, open fields were as green as a jewel. And the distant mountains still wore their snowcaps.

I didn't realize how much I'd missed my home until now. But it was not a happy homecoming. I could only think of my dead brother.

We arrived in Geneva late at night. The city gates were closed. The driver took me to a nearby inn about a mile away. But my mind was restless, and I knew I wouldn't sleep. After being in the carriage for so long, I needed to stretch my legs. So I left the inn to take a walk.

I wondered what would happen when I finally arrived in the morning. What I would say to my father? Or to Elizabeth? Or to Ernest? And our maid, Justine, must be terribly heartsick. She loved William so much.

My father had told me in his letter where they had found William's body. I felt a need to see that exact spot. I needed to see where William drew his last breath. But the place was inside the locked gates of Geneva, and the only way I could get there was to cross the lake.

I borrowed a boat from the inn and sailed across. I could see a darker sky in the distance. Storm clouds covered the moon. I knew it would be dangerous, but I would not turn back. I urged myself to move on.

It began to rain just as I pulled the boat up onto the bank. The rain fell in heavy, cool drops. I held my coat over my head for protection. Once I reached the woods, it became a downpour.

I did not turn back. I kept on until I found the spot. The grass was still stamped flat from footprints. Or was it William's body that had crushed it so? I vowed right then that I would find the murderer, even if it was the last thing I ever did.

A clap of thunder hit the sky. I needed to find shelter. Lightning zigzagged around me. Suddenly, I was overcome with a sense of gloom. Someone was watching me. I could feel it. But who else would be out in this raging storm?

I looked around but there was only darkness. The occasional light came from the flashes of lightning crossing the sky. Only trees surrounded me, and I saw nothing else. Could it be that my mind was playing tricks? No. There was someone else nearby.

I quickly turned away, ready to leave. That's when the sky lit up like a fire. And up on the hill I saw a figure. It was shaped like a man, but I knew it wasn't truly human. It was my creation. My monster.

My knees grew weak. I slumped against a tree to keep from falling.

No! I thought. *How can it be here? How did it find my home?*

The rain fell like small rocks, stinging my skin. My teeth chattered. I worried about what to do. Had it come any closer? Would I peer around the tree to see it standing there? I remembered that first night when I woke to find him by my bed.

When I finally gathered the nerve to look, he was gone. Then I knew. It had to have been the monster who killed William! He had ended my brother's life.

I could not let him roam the woods. I couldn't let him hurt someone else. I had to find him and destroy him.

I ran as quickly as I could. The rain slowed me down, but I could see where he'd been. There were broken branches and huge muddy footprints. I followed the tracks until I could see him. I raced after him. He looked back at me for a moment, and then ran away.

I tried to keep up, but couldn't. He disappeared into the brush. I felt drained. I leaned against a tree, wondering what to do next. Would I be able to find him again?

I stayed in the forest all night. My clothes and boots were soaked. My hands were rough and caked with mud. I must have looked a sight. But when the sun came up, I went back to the lake. I washed up, and then got into the boat. I rowed it back to the inn.

I walked along the road that led to my home. I tried to think of what I would say. Should I tell my family? Should I tell Elizabeth? What would she think? And what about my father? What would he say if he knew what I had done? Could he still love a son who had created a demon? Would I be blamed for William's death?

Yes, it was my fault. I had created the foul murderer. I had created the beast.

As I walked, I could see my home in the distance. The large windows reflected the morning light. It looked just the same as always. But nothing would ever be the same. Ever.

Home Again

"Victor!" my father shouted, pulling me into a hug. It was so good to see him again. The streaks of gray in his hair were now pure white. His eyes sagged with sadness. I felt terrible for having been away from him for so long.

My father lifted his chin. Tears streamed down his face. "I was hoping this would be a happy time for us," he said. "I thought when you came home we'd be having a party, not a funeral."

"I am so sorry, Father." He had no idea how much. I was truly sorry for bringing such misery to my family.

Ernest came in to greet me. "Hello, Victor."

"Ernest! It is good to see you."

He nodded and patted my back.

"How is Elizabeth?" I asked.

"She is well," he said. "All she's talked about was your return."

"And it's all I've thought about," I told him.

My father gave a small chuckle. "I think you might want to clean up before seeing her. Your clothes are damp. Your boots are covered with mud. Victor, it looks like you spent the night in the woods!"

I couldn't tell my father that I had.

The warm water and dry clothes felt like heaven. I fought to stay awake to see Elizabeth. But also because I was afraid to sleep. Sleep only brought more nightmares.

I had barely made it down the stairs when I heard, "Victor!" Her voice was like a song. Elizabeth rushed to me, and I put my arms around her. "Oh, Victor, I'm glad you've come."

Elizabeth had grown more beautiful since I'd last seen her. Her skin was like honey. Her hair looked and felt like spun gold.

"It's good to be home," I said.

"Come and have breakfast," she said, leading me to the dining room.

It seemed like forever since I'd eaten. My stomach had been tied in knots until now. But the smell of eggs and fresh fruit made me realize how hungry I was. And I enjoyed being in the company of my family once again. Father, Ernest, and Elizabeth sat with me.

"So," I said as I spread jam on my toast. "Do the police suspect anyone? Are there any clues?"

"None," Father answered. "But we're sure it was a robbery."

"Robbery?" How could that be? I was so certain my creature had killed William. But would he have robbed him as well?

Father nodded. "Yes. William always wore a locket, remember?"

"The locket with a picture of Mother?" William was so young when our mother died. Her picture was the only thing he had to remember her. He kept the locket on a chain around his neck.

"When they found William's body, the locket was missing," Elizabeth said. I could hear the sadness in her voice.

"Maybe he lost it while playing in the woods," I suggested.

"We searched," Ernest said. "A large group of people from town gathered to help. We are blessed to have so many friends."

"But I wonder why someone would want the locket," I said. "It was not really worth a lot of money. It was the picture inside that had true value, but only to our family."

"True," Father agreed, "but the robber must have thought it was valuable. What other reason would someone have to kill William?"

I had no answer for him. I knew the person who did this was a savage—a savage that I had molded with my own hands. My mind went back to the time when I robbed dead bits from graves. Back to when I pieced together the creature one part at a time. Had I been insane?

Then we heard horses coming up from the road. "We have visitors," Father said.

"Were you expecting anyone?" Ernest asked.

Father shook his head. "I was only expecting Victor, and here he sits."

There was a loud banging on the door. Someone urgently wanted to speak to us.

Father opened the door. There stood three men. Then one said, "Come quickly. They have caught the killer!"

Elizabeth and I took the carriage into town. We didn't speak the whole way. The ride seemed to take forever. My mind raced. What would I find there? Had they captured the creature? Would they have him in chains? And would he know who I am?

We pulled up to the jail. A crowd had gathered. They stomped the ground and raised their fists. "Murderer! Thief!" they shouted over and over.

"Let us through!" I ordered.

When they saw who we were, the crowd parted. Then Elizabeth and I entered.

A stout policeman came forward. "You need not worry," he said. "We've found the murderer."

"Are you sure?" I asked. I was afraid and relieved. Maybe now the monster could be destroyed.

The policeman held out the locket. "This was found in her pocket."

"Her?" I asked. I was confused. Why would they think my creation was a woman?

The policeman nodded. "She's in here."

He led us down a hall of filthy jail cells. They were filled with straw for sleeping, and each smelled like rot. I knew that smell too well.

Then we heard a cry, "Help me!" I couldn't believe it! This was the killer?

"I didn't do it!" she yelled. "I didn't do it!"

Elizabeth rushed over. I was too shocked to speak. They had captured the wrong person. They had arrested Justine!

No Justice

"Help me!" Justine cried again.

Elizabeth reached through the bars and took Justine's hand. "How did this happen?"

Justine lowered her head, weeping. "I don't know. I wasn't feeling well. I lay down in the barn and slept there all night. Next thing I know, some policemen were shaking me awake. They were holding the locket."

"But where did they find it?" I asked her.

Justine looked at me with teary eyes. "A servant said she found it. She said it fell out of my apron pocket."

"But how did it get there?" I had to know if she was guilty.

"I don't know."

We could hear the angry crowd outside.

Elizabeth looked frightened. "It sounds as if they're going to tear down the building to get in."

Through the walls we could hear them chanting, "Hang her! Hang her!"

Justine gripped the jail bars. "What am I going to do?"

I didn't know what to say. Only Elizabeth and I knew she was innocent.

The rowdy crowd banged and kicked. "Murderer! Thief! Hang her!"

"We've got to get you out of here!" Elizabeth cried. She ran back to find the policeman who'd led us to Justine.

Justine's eyes were wild with fear. She covered her ears to block out the angry shouts.

"We'll do something," I promised her.

"You'll need to hurry! Do you hear them?"

I did hear the crowd as they kicked at the door. I rushed back to make sure Elizabeth was not in danger. Several policemen were holding off the mob.

"Go home!" one policeman shouted toward the crowd. "You can have your say during the trial."

They continued to shout.

"I said go home!" the policeman ordered. Soon the crowd broke up and left the jail.

I helped Elizabeth to the carriage. She buried her face in her hands, crying.

I leaned back into the seat, my face burning with guilt. They would surely hang her. Soon Justine would be dead, and that would be two murders I had caused. Poor William. Poor Justine. How could I have done this to them? How could I have known?

We delivered the news to my father once we were home. He sat back, shaking his head.

"Do you think she killed William?" he asked.

"No, Father," I answered. "Justine was innocent."

"Then who?" Father wondered.

I did not know what to say. Should I tell him that I had created a murderer? Would he listen? Would he believe me? Would he hate me?

⚜

Justine was brought before the magistrate, and her trial began. One woman said that Justine must be guilty because she had stayed out all night. Another said she saw Justine that morning near the spot where William had been murdered.

There was talk of the locket and how it came to be in Justine's apron. The people were angry, fully believing that she was guilty.

Then Elizabeth took the stand to testify. She told the court that Justine was a kind and loving person, and that she would never hurt a soul.

Father testified too. He spoke of Justine as though she were his own daughter. He recalled all the wonderful things she had done for the family.

I also spoke on her behalf. I insisted that she could not have done such a ghastly thing. I wanted to confess to them who the real killer was, but I couldn't.

The magistrate asked Justine if she had done it. "No," she cried. "I am innocent. I loved William."

But soon the verdict was read. "Guilty!"

We went home knowing there was nothing else we could do. They would hang Justine.

I cried throughout the night. What have I done? How can I live with myself after this? I thought I might go completely insane.

A few days later my father said, "I think we should get away for a while. This house only holds sadness for us."

I agreed that it was a wonderful idea. Getting away would make us all feel a little better.

My father owned another home several miles away. I had not been there in a good while. So we packed our things and left.

I had forgotten how lovely the mountains and valleys were. In the early morning, the mountains near this home were the same color as the sky. I loved it here. But I was still having nightmares. I continued to see the monster over and over in my sleep. And my dreams were filled with Justine's agonizing cries.

Most nights I would wander away, taking the boat out on the lake. I would let the wind carry me as the boat sailed freely on the water. I didn't care where it led.

Both Elizabeth and Father noticed my sadness. "Victor," Father said, "I thought coming here would cheer you up?"

I shook my head. "My mind is so mixed up. We lost William. We lost Justine."

"But it's time to put those things behind us," he said.

I couldn't. Not as long as the creature lived. I was confused. Should I go after it? I didn't even know where it had hidden. Could it still be in Geneva?

I went to Elizabeth. Our days here had made her cheeks rosier. She seemed to breathe easier.

"Elizabeth, I'm going away for a bit."

She looked shocked. "Away? Where are you going?"

"I have to be alone for a bit," I told her. "I need some time to think."

She placed her hand in mine. "It breaks my heart, but I understand. So much has happened. Where will you go?"

"The mountain."

"But why would you want to go there?" she asked. "You are likely to freeze on the mountain."

I didn't know how to explain. "I think the climb will help me."

Elizabeth nodded. "Do what you think is right. I'll be waiting."

"I will be back as soon as I can," I promised.

I took my heavy coat and boots. I packed

some bread and fruit. Then I gave Elizabeth a long hug.

"Take care of Father," I said to her.

"I will. But please return quickly."

I told her I would even though I didn't know when I would be back. I would stay as long as it took. I had to breathe the crisp mountain air. I had to clear the black thoughts from my head.

And so I headed out. I walked and walked without stopping. I stared up at the mountain, knowing it would be a long climb. I didn't care. It was something I had to do.

What I didn't know then was that I would come face-to-face with my worst nightmare!

The Mountain

The road stretched long before me. I could feel the dirt crunching under my boots. I took in the beauty of it all. The greens of the valleys were pleasant and pure. They swept across the base of the mountains. The pine trees stood tall and firm; their needles sprinkled the ground. The wind blew softly.

As I passed the cottages, I thought how nice it would be to live a simple life. The people inside were not worried about death or menace or monsters.

I continued on. The mountain stood before me like an enormous fortress. I knew I couldn't make it all the way up on foot.

A farmer loaned me one of his mules. The mule carried my pack.

As I reached the mountain the road changed. I was no longer walking on soft earth. It had become rough and rocky. We stepped around jagged stones and prickly branches.

I looked up a few times, no longer able to see the mountaintop. But that didn't stop me. I knew I had a long journey ahead.

I would stop by the mountain streams for water, and then I'd rest for a while. The mule was my only companion.

After a few days, the road narrowed. It grew sharper and uneven. The cliffs had become dangerous. I knew the mule couldn't make it. I let it loose so it could head back down to safety.

I didn't mind the climb. It was something I was compelled to do. As long as I was straining to get to the top, my mind was free. I only thought of moving on. Instead of thinking

about William or Justine, I concentrated on my journey. One slip and I was doomed.

A few times I had to dodge rock slides. Pebbles dropped down on me, biting my skin. A few of the larger rocks would pound my shoulders. I covered my head as best I could.

My clothes were soiled, but I had no time to change. And I only rested when I needed food and water. No matter how hard the trek, I kept moving.

Soon the nights grew colder. I bundled up, pulling my coat tight around me. I would camp under an overhang in the cliff. But then the days grew colder, too. The crunching of dirt and rock under my footsteps became the soft crunch of snow.

The wind burned my hands right through my gloves. Sometimes I would stop to empty snow from my boots. But I breathed in the cold mountain air, and it felt crisp and good.

I wondered how far I had to climb. Would I make it to the top? Would I die here? I didn't care. I wanted so badly to change the past. I wanted things to be as they were when I was much younger.

Again I thought of my mother. She had been so young and beautiful, just like the picture in the locket. How unfair that she had to die too soon.

I thought about William. He always looked a lot like Mother. He had her soft, brown hair and hazel eyes. I'm sure my father thought about Mother every time he'd looked at William. But now, William was dead. Father only had pictures of my mother to remind him.

I thought about Justine, and how unfair life can be. Poor Justine. In my mind I could see the heavy rope, thick and strong and rough. I couldn't bear the thought of it around her neck. How frightened she must have been in the end.

Even in the bitter cold I went on. I would sometimes look down at the valley below. I could only see the pointed treetops of the pines. The roads and cottages were too far away now.

But I knew somewhere down there that birds were singing. I seemed to be the only breathing creature up here.

It became harder and harder to move. It felt like my boots were filled with heavy stones. But then, I saw it. I saw the very top. I had done it. I had made the climb all the way up.

I sat down on the ground, smiling to myself. What now? Would the cold mountain air really clear my dark thoughts? Would life be normal again when I returned?

Then I saw something out of the corner of my eye. Something fast was moving toward me. I jumped up, frightened.

"Who's there?" I yelled.

It kept coming in my direction. It was a man. He was huge! His coat covered most of his body. But I soon realized it was no man. It was him. It was the monster.

I remembered the look on his face as he stood by my bed. Should I be frightened? Had he come here to kill me?

I picked up a large branch to use as a weapon. If he charged at me, I'd swing it. But he slowed down as he got closer. He looked different.

Time had made him uglier. His hair had grown long and shaggy. It hung in knotted tangles upon his shoulders. Where I had stitched his face now had huge purple scars. His lips were thin and blue, and his eyes were like slits above his crooked nose.

"Frankenstein!" he roared.

I couldn't believe it. He talked! The monster had said my name.

"Frankenstein," he repeated.

I was astounded. "You can speak?"

He nodded. "Yes, I can speak."

"But I don't understand. Where have you been? How did you learn the language?"

He pointed one fat, stubby finger at me. "You left me!" he yelled. "You made me, and then you left me alone!"

"It was a mistake!" I cried. "A mistake!"

"And this is how you correct your mistakes?" he asked. "By running away from them?"

"I'm so sorry," I said.

"It is too late to apologize. You abandoned me."

I was curious. I had to know. "Where did you go? What have you been doing all this time?"

The creature looked down at me with hatred in his eyes and said, "Sit down."

"But . . . but," I stuttered.

He shoved me hard. "Sit down!"

I landed hard on the snow. He crouched next to me. "I will tell you of the horrors I have faced."

The Monster's Story

The monster looked around. He saw me shivering on the ground. "Come," he said.

He led me to a cave of ice. Inside it we were sheltered from the wind. The creature made a fire. I was amazed at his ability.

"I have much to tell," he said to me. "We need to stay warm."

I moved close to the fire. It was the first time in days that I did not shiver. It felt good.

The monster sat near me. "You left me," he said.

I didn't know what to say. I was confused.

"You created me and then left me alone!" he roared.

"What happened to you? Tell me."

The monster held his hands to the fire. "After you ran away, I didn't know what to do. I felt dizzy and hungry. I took one of your coats and some gloves and left your apartment. I needed food. The rain drenched me, and I was so cold. But I walked the dark streets.

"I followed some scurrying rats because I thought they might lead me to food. I ended up behind the inn. There was a bin of garbage there. I found a half-eaten apple and a shriveled potato inside. I fought the rats for it. Then I found shelter by the back door of the inn. When morning came I heard a stirring inside. I thought maybe I could beg for food.

"The innkeeper opened the door. When he saw me he screamed and slammed the door in my face. I ran off through the back alley. It was empty. There was no food.

"Soon I came to a clearing. Some children were playing outside. When they saw me they fled. Some adults came out of their houses and shouted. They threw rocks and sticks at me.

They called me 'monster' and 'beast.' I hurried away into the woods.

"I wandered about for a day, eating berries and nuts. Then I followed some animals to a stream. My throat was dry and parched. I watched the animals drink. I lay down to lap up the water. But that's when I saw . . ."

The monster stopped speaking and looked at me with pure hatred.

"Saw what?" I asked him.

"I saw my reflection. There was blood on my face. Many of the stitches you had used to piece me together had broken. I saw my huge, crooked nose and twisted mouth. I knew then why people were afraid. I was the ugliest creature on Earth.

"I drank from the stream, but I was so bitterly cold. I spent days walking through the forest. Then one day, I came upon a campfire that had been left burning. I enjoyed the warmth. I put my hand into it, but it burned! Then I stayed near it for the heat.

"I noticed that there was some meat left near the fire. It had been cooked. So I took a bite. It tasted wonderful. But soon I worried that the fire might go out.

"I studied it and saw that the fire had been built with wood. I gathered some branches to keep the flames from dying out. Then I learned how to cook meat and roast nuts over it. When I ran out of food, I could only find acorns on the ground. I knew I had to move on.

"I walked for several days, and then I saw a cabin up ahead. I knew I would be warm inside. But there were people there. I hid in a small room filled with hay. It was built onto the cabin. There was a small hole in the wall, and when I peeked in, I could see the family going about their business.

"After watching them for days, I learned many things. There was an older man. He was blind. They called him *Father*. There was a sweet girl named Agatha and a son named Felix.

"They were always kind to each other. And at night, the father would play music on his guitar. It was such a sweet sound.

"But I was hungry, so while they slept I would steal their food. That caused them to wake up unhappy. It made me unhappy, too.

"I began to love this family. I would listen to them talk. I learned many words from them. Soon I could speak full sentences. Then I would sneak their books, which helped me learn to read and write. Watching them taught me so much.

"The more I observed them, the sadder I became because they were so poor. So I went out one night and cut firewood for them and left it by their door. When they woke the next morning, they looked around to see who could have left it. Then they brought it inside. Now they had plenty of firewood for heat and cooking.

"For the first time, I felt good about myself. I had done something to bring happiness. So I would go out at night and find berries and nuts and leave those for the family, too. They would always search, but they never knew who was leaving the small gifts for them.

"For a year I stayed there. I only watched the family through the hole in the wall. But I hated just watching. I wanted to be a part of it all.

"One day, when Agatha and Felix had gone out, I went to the door. The father was alone. 'Come in,' he told me. So I entered the house for the first time. The father gave me food, and then he sat with his guitar. He sang the most wonderful songs. I loved him so much.

"But then, Felix and Agatha returned. They saw me. Agatha screamed. Felix yelled, 'You monster!' He picked up a log and beat me. He chased me out of the cabin.

"I shielded myself and ran away. I could have fought, but I wouldn't dare hurt Felix. I owed the family so much. Because of them, I had learned to read and write and speak.

"I knew I couldn't return. They hated me. Everyone hated me. I decided then, that I would also hate. I vowed to never be kind to anyone.

"I walked through the woods again. One night I stopped to make a fire. Sitting close, I put my hands into the pocket of my coat. It was the coat I had taken from your home. Inside I found some papers. They had always been there, but I had never known how to read them until then.

"So I took them out and read. And the more

I read, the angrier I became. I knew why people called me monster and beast. And I knew exactly what I had to do!"

The Monster's Demands

"You read my papers?" I asked. I was still shocked that my creation could read at all.

"Yes," the monster said. "Through your notes I learned how you created me. I read how you had robbed graveyards and sewn me together with parts from dead bodies. I could only assume that you were insane."

"Yes," I agreed. "I know that now."

"But look at me!" the monster demanded. "You caused this!" He pointed to his face.

I closed my eyes. I didn't want to see. I didn't want to face the truth.

"I knew I had to find you," he said.

"Did you come to kill me?" I asked.

He only glared at me as I waited for him to speak. "No," he said at last. "I have other plans for you."

"But you are a murderer. You killed my brother and our housemaid."

The monster nodded. "I hated you for what you had done."

"Then why didn't you come for me? Why kill innocent people?"

"I loathed you so much," he said. "After reading your papers, I knew where I needed to go. I walked for days to find you at your home in Geneva."

"But I wasn't there," I said.

The monster's lips curved into a wicked smile. "I wasn't sure if you would be there or not. But I knew how to bring you home."

"What exactly did you do?"

"I continued on," he said. "I walked without stopping. The closer I got to Geneva, the more hatred I felt for you. It ate me up. But I needed you. Then when I came to the woods outside your home, I saw a boy running about."

"My brother."

He nodded. "I didn't know that then. I loved watching him. He was so full of life. He would chase the squirrels and climb trees. He threw rocks into the stream to watch them tap across the water. He was having so much fun."

"My brother loved to play," I said.

"Yes, I could tell. He smiled as he ran. He seemed extremely happy."

"Then why did you kill him?" I asked.

"I didn't mean to," he said. "I only wanted to talk to him. I wanted to know if I was on the right path. But when he saw me, he screamed. He ran away. I chased him through the woods, but he ran so fast."

"Yes," I agreed. "He could outrun all of us."

The monster looked down, watching the flames of the fire. "I couldn't let him get away. But he was too far ahead. Then he tripped on

some fallen branches. When I came close, he backed away. He wouldn't stop screaming."

I buried my face in my hands. "What did you do?" I mumbled.

"I wasn't planning to kill him," the monster said. "I only asked him if he knew where I could find the house of Frankenstein. His eyes grew big. His voice stuttered. 'Yes, I know,' he said to me. 'I am a Frankenstein.'"

I raised my head to look at this beast. "Did he beg for his life?"

"Not at first," the monster answered. "But I was enraged. I wanted to punish you for what you had done. I remembered my pretend family. I had loved those whom I had watched for so long. Then I remembered how they had treated me. I wanted you to feel that pain."

I knew then that William had been killed to punish me. "What happened next?"

"I moved toward him," the monster said. "He was frightened. He asked me to go away. He pleaded with me not to hurt him. But I couldn't help it. I knew that you loved him. I knew he was your brother, so I picked the boy up and shook him. I shook him and shook him and shook him so hard."

The monster stopped speaking.

"Go on!" I pleaded. "Tell me what happened!"

"The boy pounded against my chest. He shouted hateful things at me. He kicked at me.

He called me a monster. But I kept on shaking and shaking him. He continued to scream.

"I put my hand over his mouth to try and stop him. Soon, his kicking ceased. His arms dropped to his side. I knew then that he was dead. So I laid him down upon the ground."

"And the locket?" I asked. "Did you take it?"

"Yes," he said, "I took it. I didn't want anyone coming after me. I had to find someone else to take the blame. So I wandered through the woods until I came to a path. I could see a large house up ahead. I somehow knew it was your home."

I imagined the monster lurking around my family. I thought of how close he had come to my father and Elizabeth. Should I be thankful that he hadn't killed them too?

"I stopped in the barn to rest. I thought I might find some eggs to eat, or maybe a chicken I could kill and cook. But when I walked in, I was surprised to see a lovely young woman sleeping on the straw."

"Justine," I said. "Her name was Justine."

"I didn't care who she was. I only knew that I had to find someone to take the blame for the boy's death. And I realized that she was probably someone you cared about."

"You were right," I said. "She was not just our housemaid. She was like a sister to us."

His lips turned into an evil smile. "All the better."

"So you placed the locket in her apron?" I asked.

"Of course. And it worked. They came for her instead of me."

I considered all that he had told me. I hung my head. I had come to this mountain to find peace, but instead I'd found more misery.

"When I first came home," I said, "you saw me in the woods. Why didn't you kill me then?"

"I have no plans to kill you, Frankenstein. As I said before, I need you. I am sick of being alone," he said. "I want you to make me a wife."

A Proposal

"A wife?" I asked. "Never! Do not ask me to do this!"

He glared at me with hatred. "You will."

I couldn't go through that physical pain again. All that time and agony.

"I can't. It would be far too much work," I explained. "I don't think I'm capable of reproducing my work."

His lip curled into a snarl. "You did it once. You can do it again."

"And then what?" I asked. "Would I be creating another murderer?"

Sparks flew into the air as the monster stirred the fire. "You don't understand. I killed those people for a reason."

"Yes, I do understand," I said. "You killed them to get back at me. You wanted me to feel pain. And you have certainly succeeded."

"It was more than that," he told me.

"Then explain it to me. There is no reason to kill."

He stared into the burning embers. "I was lonely. I only wanted a friend. I wanted just one person to care about me."

For once I felt some pity for him.

"I was sick of people being frightened or cruel. I was angry. And the one person who should have loved me turned away."

For the first time, I saw him express sadness.

"You should have loved me as a son," he went on. "You were my father. It was you who created me. And yet, you ran away. You left me all alone to search for food and shelter. I had to learn all my skills on my own. And now, you will make that up to me."

I thought about what he was saying. It had been wrong for me to leave him. But then, it had also been wrong for me to create him. And what about this new creation that he wanted? Would she frighten people as well? Would they throw things at her and scream when she came near?

"How will you make your way in the world?" I asked him. "It is one thing for you to look after yourself. But you would have to look after your wife as well. People will not change. They won't accept you or her."

"I have a plan," he told me. "Once you have made my bride, I will take her away."

"Where?" I asked. "People are the same no matter where you go."

"I will take her to South America. I read that there are many jungles there. Places where no man has even set foot. She and I would live there all alone. We would have each other for company. We wouldn't need anyone else."

I contemplated what he asked. Could I spend another year away from my family?

"And what happens if I refuse?" I asked.

His eyes burned into me. "Then one by one, those you love will die, and you will be left alone. Then you will know how it feels. And you will weep for what you had done to me."

"And if I build you a wife, will you promise to go away and leave my family in peace? And will you promise that I will never see you again?"

The monster nodded. "You have my word."

"Then I must get back to my laboratory. I will begin soon as possible. But first I need to say good-bye to my family."

The monster nodded in agreement as he kicked snow onto the fire, causing it to hiss. "Remember your promise, Frankenstein. I will give you one year."

Then he stood and walked away, leaving me alone in the cold.

 ⚝

I traveled back down the mountain to my family. Elizabeth greeted me at the door. "Oh, Victor, we've been so worried!"

Father hurried over. "Son, you look so pale and thin. Come have something to eat."

I sat down at the table as Elizabeth brought me tea and cakes. "Here," she said. "Now tell us about your journey."

Father leaned forward. He was eager to hear.

"I made it to top of the mountain," I said.

"And did it clear you mind?" Father asked.

I couldn't tell him the truth—that what I had found on that mountain had caused me even more pain.

"Relax. Eat," Elizabeth said. "You can tell us later. We're just happy to have you home."

After my meal I lay down to sleep, but I couldn't rest for long. I had work to do. And I had an important decision.

Later, I met Elizabeth out in the garden.

"I have to go away again," I told her. I knew she'd be hurt by my leaving again.

"No, Victor," she said. "You mustn't leave. Your place is with us." Tears formed in her eyes.

"But this is something I have to do. I have no choice."

"Why? What is it?" she asked. "Please tell me."

I couldn't.

"Please, Victor. You've been away far too much. I can't bear for you to leave me again."

"And I can't bear being away from you, but believe me when I say it's something I have to do."

She hung her head as tears rolled down her cheeks.

I took her hands in mine. "I'll be gone for a year," I told her. "But when I return, everything will be fine. And then I want us to marry."

She looked up at me. Her face brightened. "Really?"

"Oh, yes. I want to marry you more than anything. But it must wait for now."

She smiled. "I love you, Victor. I will count the days till you return."

"And then I'll never leave you again."

She threw her arms around me. I hugged her tight. I knew that once I left, it would be a long, long time before I would see her again. But I would be done with monsters and murder. And there would be no more nightmares; no more sleepless nights. Elizabeth and I would marry and be happy forever.

I told Father of my plans to leave. His face showed worry. "I don't want you to go alone."

"I must," I said.

Father shook his head. "Stay a few more days. I will write to your friend, Henry. He'll go with you back to England."

Back to the Graveyard

Henry and I left for England. It was a long journey, and we spent days talking of old times. He constantly wanted to know how I was feeling.

I didn't tell him much. I couldn't. He filled the silence by telling me about his studies, his eyes bright when he spoke. He was always cheerful. I envied him. I didn't think I could ever be that happy again. But I was glad that I had my good friend here to keep my mind off my future work.

Once we were in England, I visited a scientist who knew much about the workings of the female body. Building a woman would be much different than creating a man. I had to make sure everything would work perfectly. He taught me a great deal. I took detailed notes. From time to time he would ask about my project, but I said very little. I knew he would laugh if I told him the truth. He would never believe me.

Henry spent his time studying different languages. He stayed busy and didn't bother me. I was happy for that.

I built my new laboratory. I only worked when Henry was not around. I gathered supplies, and soon my lab was filled with the things I needed. The tables were lined with instruments and jars.

But I had to be careful. I couldn't let Henry know what I was doing. He would think I was insane. Sometimes I thought maybe I was.

Luckily, Henry received a letter from a friend, asking us to come to Scotland. He begged me to go, but I couldn't put off my project any longer. Time was running short.

"Please," Henry said. "It will be fun."

"I can't," I told him. I had no time for fun.

Henry agreed to go without me, and I began my gruesome work.

Just as I had before, I sneaked into the graveyards at night. I collected what I needed. It was much harder this time. I was weaker. I had not taken care of myself.

I didn't want to stop, but many times I had to sit down for fear of falling over from hunger. My mind was only on this creation.

To make it easier, I thought about Elizabeth. I pictured her in the garden surrounded by beautiful roses and clinging vines. I imagined our wedding day and how happy we would be.

I placed the body pieces on the table. I stitched and sewed. Sometimes a part wasn't quite right. It was too long or too short. But many times it was because it had begun to rot.

When the sun set, I would work by candlelight. I rarely even knew what time it was. It didn't matter. Only the task at hand was important.

I rarely went out. And I spoke to no one. I was so lonely. I wanted to write to Elizabeth and my father, but I wasn't sure what to say. I couldn't tell them what I was doing.

And so I pressed on. Hours went by. Then days. Then months. I had finally completed the body. All I needed now was a thunderstorm.

I placed a lightning rod on the roof. I hooked a wire to the creature. Days later, a storm rolled in that shook the entire city.

I waited, wondering if it would work again. How would it be with this creation? Would she be a wild, vicious animal? Would she really learn to love the monster? These questions rolled through my mind and filled me with doubt.

Just before a streak of lightning could hit the rod, I rolled the table away, pulling the wire loose. I couldn't do it! I couldn't make the same horrendous mistake.

I sat with my head in my hands. But then I had a feeling that someone was watching me. I looked toward the window. It was him! The monster had been watching me the whole time!

He crashed in and grabbed me by the throat. "Why did you stop?" he roared. "Finish this!"

"No! I can't!"

The monster threw me to the floor. "You have failed me, Frankenstein! If I can't be happy, then neither can you! Remember this— I will see you on your wedding night!"

He turned and stomped away.

So that was his plan. He would not murder me now. He would wait until I had some hope of happiness, and then he would kill me.

⊰⊱

The next day I stuffed the body of the female creature into a large bag and took it down to the beach. It was heavy so I had to drag it along.

I made sure no one was watching as I placed it into a boat. Then I rowed out to sea. The waves were strong, making it hard to navigate. But I wouldn't stop.

I went as far out as the small boat would take me. Then, when I was sure it was safe, I dumped the body overboard. It sank quickly to the bottom. The fish could have it now. No one would ever know what I had done. I could go back to Geneva and marry Elizabeth. And I would do everything I could to keep the monster away.

I was so tired and weak that I lay down in the boat. I hadn't had any sleep. I couldn't keep my eyes open. I drifted off, and so did the boat.

When I woke up, I realized that the boat had sailed off to a strange island. I wasn't sure where I was.

When I rowed to shore, a crowd was waiting. They watched as my small boat got closer and closer. What did they want from me? Did they know what I had done?

I could tell it was me that they wanted. They pointed and shouted. Their faces were twisted in anger. Something was wrong. Suddenly, I was afraid.

When I pulled the boat up on the sand, some men came forward.

"What's your name?" one of them asked.

"Victor Frankenstein."

"Mr. Frankenstein, you are under arrest." The man came forward and grabbed my arm. "For murder."

Prison

The men roughly tugged me along. "We're taking you to see Mr. Kirwin, the judge."

"But I'm innocent!" I pleaded. They had the wrong man. I hadn't murdered anyone.

They took me to a home in the middle of town. A stout man stood before us. "Here he is, Mr. Kirwin," the man said gruffly. "He's the murderer."

"But I didn't do it! I was at my apartment all night. Then today, I rowed out to do some fishing." I had no choice but to lie. "My boat drifted here."

Mr. Kirwin scratched his chin.

"A body was found on the beach," another man said. "We saw his boat on the water."

The gruff man who had dragged me away spoke up, "It had to be him. He's a stranger."

"Yes," another man said. "No one else here would have committed such a crime."

"You have to believe me," I begged. "I didn't do it."

Their eyes narrowed. It was no use. They would never believe me. Then Mr. Kirwin said, "Let's show him the body. We'll be able to tell by his reaction if he's the murderer."

They led me off to a small room where a body lay upon a wooden table. The body was covered with a white sheet. One of the men shoved me inside. "Take a look," he growled.

I had to be careful. I had to show that I was innocent. I slowly walked forward and waited. The man nodded, and then another pulled back the sheet.

No! I grew dizzy and fell to the ground, kicking and crying. The man on the table was Henry Clerval!

The monster! He had murdered Henry.

It was too much for me. Everything went black, and I passed out there on the floor. I didn't remember much after that. My body raged with fever.

When I finally woke up, I looked around, wondering where I was. Then I saw the bars in front of me. I was in prison! But for how long?

I sat up, rubbing my face. My clothes were covered in filth. My hands were grubby and rough, and I had a foul taste in my mouth. I needed water.

"Ah, you're awake at last," a woman said.

I turned toward the voice. It was a nurse sitting in the corner of the cell. She brought me a dipper of water, and then felt my forehead. "Your fever is gone."

"How long have I been here?" I asked.

"Two months," she told me.

Two months! What had gone on while I was sleeping? Was the monster nearby? Had he returned to kill my family?

"I must get out of here," I said to the nurse.

She laughed. "I don't think that's possible. Now that you're better, they can proceed with the trial."

I lay back down on my bed. A trial? The townspeople still thought I was guilty. They would never believe that a monster I had created killed Henry.

I felt sick all over again. I covered my face and cried. The nurse used her key to slip out of the cell. "I must go and tell the judge that you're awake."

Then I was alone again.

Later that day, the judge came in. "Mr. Frankenstein, you are looking much better."

I sat up. "Why was there a nurse here?" I asked. "If you think I murdered Henry, then why didn't you just let me die?"

"Because I don't really think you're guilty," he said.

For the first time I had some hope. The judge was on my side. "Why do you think that?" I wondered.

He held out a letter. "While you were sick, we looked through your things. This was in your pocket."

I took it from him. It was a letter I'd received from Henry.

"This man must have been your friend," Mr. Kirwin said.

"Yes," I agreed. "He was my best friend."

Mr. Kirwin's eyes softened. "I don't see any reason why you would kill him."

"I didn't," I said. "I could never hurt Henry."

"Yes," Mr. Kirwin said. "But the townspeople are still accusing you."

I still felt a bit better knowing the judge believed me. "What about my family? Do they know where I am?"

Mr. Kirwin put his hand on my shoulder. "I wrote to them. They are concerned. Your father is on his way here."

I sat back, wiping my straggly hair away from my face. My heart felt lighter. Father was coming. He would take care of things.

It was only a few days later when Father arrived. I was never so happy to see anyone in my life.

"Victor!" he shouted when he saw me. "We were so sad to hear about Henry."

"I didn't do it, Father."

"Of course you didn't," he said. "I've brought good news. We've found someone to speak at your trial. He'd given Henry's letter to you at the same time Henry was murdered. He knows it couldn't have been you."

I grabbed Father's hand through the cell bars. "Thank you," I said.

It was several weeks before my trial began. I had been in prison for three full months. But the jury believed the witness, and I was set free. I could now go back to Geneva and marry Elizabeth.

Father thought I was too weak to travel, but I insisted. I had to get home. I knew that everyone was safe. For now.

The Wedding

My father and I journeyed back to Geneva. The trip seemed to take forever. I wanted to see Elizabeth. She had waited for me all this time.

I tried not to think of the monster. I knew he'd be there somewhere, hiding and waiting for me.

"What is troubling you, son?" Father asked.

He could see the worry on my face. "I don't know how to explain it," I said.

He watched me closely. "You are free, Victor. We are on our way home. You never need to leave again."

I knew he was right, but I still felt so guilty. "Father, I am so sorry."

"For what?" he asked.

"William is dead. Justine is dead. And now Henry is dead. It's all my fault."

"Don't say that," Father said. "How can you be at fault? Victor, you cannot blame yourself."

I buried my face in my hands. "Trust me. I caused all of this."

"But how?"

I sat quietly, wondering how I could explain. Should I tell him about the hours spent in the lab? How would he feel if he knew I had dug up graves and removed the dead?

"I don't know how to begin," I told him. I wanted to tell him so badly. I felt I might go insane if I didn't tell someone! But what would he think? What would he do? And if he did know, would the monster take revenge on him as well?

"I can't," I said to him.

"Very well," he said. "When you feel you are ready, you can tell me then. But I don't think you should be blaming yourself."

I didn't reply. I couldn't. I spent the rest of the journey thinking of Elizabeth. I pictured her beautiful smile. That is what got me through it. That is what gave me a bit of hope.

When we arrived, Elizabeth met me at the door. "Oh Victor, I've been so worried about you!" She threw her arms around me.

"No need to worry now," I said. "I'm home."

Tears came to her eyes. "I thought I might have lost you. I wrote to Mr. Kirwin and thanked him for providing a nurse for you. I wanted to come when I heard you were sick."

"I'm glad you didn't," I said. "I wouldn't have wanted you to see me like that."

She wiped away some tears. "And poor Henry. Why would someone want to kill him?"

I had no answer for her. If I told her about the monster I created, then she would think me a monster too.

"Let's not dwell on it," I told her. "Let's just think of the happy times ahead."

She nodded in agreement. Then she smiled. "Yes, there will be happy times. I'm so thrilled that you're home."

After that, I spent my days with Elizabeth. We took long walks or sat in the garden, talking about our future. We had not set a date for our wedding. I kept thinking about the monster's threat. He planned to kill me. I felt him waiting and watching. He knew that the day would come when Elizabeth and I would marry. I was afraid.

But Elizabeth grew impatient. She never said it, but I knew she was eager to get married. And I wanted her to be happy.

Then one day in the garden, I took her hands in mine. "Elizabeth, it is time. Will you marry me?"

She threw her arms around me. "Yes! Yes, Victor." She was filled with joy.

The next few weeks were spent with wedding plans. We arranged for a minister, flowers, and a cake. Many people were invited.

"Victor," Elizabeth said, "are you all right? You don't seem happy about our wedding."

"I am," I told her. "But there is a secret in my past. A secret I cannot reveal until after we are married."

She didn't press me for an answer. Our wedding day was so close. She would wait until then.

I tried to think of how I might explain it to her. She would have to know. And since the monster planned to kill me, I needed to do whatever I could to stay safe.

When the day finally came, we said our marriage vows. Elizabeth's cheeks were rosy, and she smiled the entire time. I had never seen her look so beautiful.

When it was time to depart, we took a carriage to the family cottage. I told no one where we were going.

"Victor, this was the happiest day of my life!" Elizabeth said, as we entered the cottage. "And there will be so many happy days to come."

I wanted to believe her. Surely the monster would not find us here.

We walked together around the cottage grounds. The flowers were blooming. It was breathtaking. But then I worried. What if my creature did come to find me?

My worries grew as night fell. "Elizabeth, I want you to stay inside. I will be back shortly."

"Where are you going?" she asked.

"Just to check the grounds. I want to make sure everything is secure."

I walked around the cottage. I heard only the sounds of the night. The crickets chirped. The frogs croaked. I saw nothing that should concern me.

But that's when I heard a piercing scream. It was Elizabeth! I rushed back into the cottage. "Elizabeth!" I shrieked. "Elizabeth!"

I found her lying on the floor. Her face was twisted in horror. I fell to my knees in agony. My poor Elizabeth was dead!

A Final Vow

"No!" I screamed, pulling Elizabeth into my arms. How could I have not seen the truth! The monster had said, *I will be with you on your wedding night.* But it was not me he meant to kill. It was my precious Elizabeth.

I rushed out into the night, looking everywhere. Then I heard him. He was laughing at me. I tried searching for him, but he was too quick.

"I will get you!" I vowed. "I will hunt you down and destroy you!"

I spent the next few days in grief and anger. I wrote to Father, telling him I would be home soon. When the final arrangements had been made, I went back to Geneva.

Father lay in bed. His face was pale. His hands shook. It had all been too much for him. First he lost William, and now Elizabeth. She had been like a daughter to him.

"Victor," he said, his voice weak, "why has this happened to us?"

I only hung my head. I would not make it worse by confessing the truth. I stayed by my father's side as his sickness grew worse. I knew there was no hope. And when he closed his eyes for the last time, I knew he had died of heartache.

I had nothing left. Everyone I loved was gone. But why should they be dead while the monster lived?

I went to the town magistrate to explain. "We have to find Elizabeth's killer," I said. "I know who he is."

"Then tell me," he said.

So I did. I told him everything that I had done. How I had created a man. And how that creation had murdered my family.

The magistrate laughed. "Victor Frankenstein, you expect me to believe that? Now leave. I will hear no more of your ranting."

I could not convince him. I knew then that this was something I had to do alone.

I needed revenge, so I left Geneva in search of the monster. I followed his trail. It was difficult at first, but he left small clues. Then I realized that he wanted me to find him. But he made a game of it and was always one step ahead of me.

My anger grew. Some days I would shout, "Come out and face me! Stop leading me on! Let's finish this now!" But he never showed himself. Sometimes he left messages. Sometimes he left objects. They always led me a little closer, but not close enough.

I followed him northward. The chill winds cut through me, and soon I found myself crossing ice and snow. Why here? Did he know that the frost would weaken me? The monster was much bigger and stronger than I. He could have killed me at any time. But still we journeyed north.

I found that I could no longer follow on foot. I purchased a sled and dogs to carry me. Some nights I feared I might freeze to death. The only thing keeping me alive was my hatred for him.

I vowed to kill him, and I would keep my promise. I had to do it for William, Justine, Henry, and my father. But most of all, I had to do it for my beloved Elizabeth.

I kept on even when my dogs were dying one by one. But then, I hit the jagged ice. My sled broke into several pieces. I was too cold and weak to continue. So I gave up, ready to die too.

And that is when I saw your ship, Captain Walton. That is when you found me. You have been so kind. But please promise me one thing. When I die, find my monster. Find him and kill him. Do it for me, please. Even in death, I will not rest if he is alive.

Captain Walton

I listen as Victor Frankenstein finishes his story. It is an unbelievable tale, and yet I believe him. "You are safe now. No need to dwell on it," I tell him.

He lays his head back on the pillow.

Some crewmen come in, bringing us food and tea. But Victor refuses to eat. I can see the light growing weak in his eyes. I know what he is thinking. Somewhere out there is a hideous creature. A creature that is so horrible, no one can bear to look at him.

Should I be afraid? I want to ask Victor, but he's fallen asleep. Telling his story has weakened him even more.

A crewman enters. "Captain Walton, the men grow weary. We must turn our ship around and head back to England. We have waited too long."

He is right. I cannot put it off any longer. It is time to turn back.

I leave Victor on his bed inside the cabin. I know his health is poor, but I can check on him again later. It is time for me to tend to my ship.

We spend many hours working to pry the ship out of the mountain of ice. It is a difficult task. Many men suffer from frostbite. Others are near death. I try my best to keep them safe, but we are in a difficult position.

Yet we manage and strain until we are no longer trapped in the ice. And soon we can sail back home.

My men shout with joy. "We've done it! We're free!"

I hurry back to the cabin to tell Victor of our success. I will promise to find him the best doctors in England. He will grow strong again.

But when I enter, I see an astonishing sight. Next to Victor's bed stands a large, beastly creature. I know right then that Victor had told the truth, for his monster has come aboard our ship.

The creature's face is scarred and deformed. His crooked nose and twisted mouth send chills through me. We stare at each other for a moment. Then I see tears in his eyes.

"He is dead," the creature says, pointing to Victor.

"You should be happy," I tell him. "Isn't that what you wanted?"

"No," he says. "I wanted him to care for me. He created me. He should have looked after me. But he left me alone, and I had to endure the hatred of the world."

"But you punished him," I say.

The monster bends down by Victor's body and weeps. "I wanted him to feel the pain that I felt. I wanted him to know what it was like.

But now I am sorry for what I have done. Forgive me, Frankenstein."

The monster hugs Victor's body against him.

"What will you do now?" I ask.

The monster doesn't answer. He lays Frankenstein's body back onto the bed. "Farewell, Frankenstein. Now that you are dead, there is no reason for me to live."

The monster rushes to the window and jumps out.

"Wait!" I cry, hurrying over. But the monster continues crossing the ice. Soon the waves of the ocean sweep up, and the creature disappears into them.

We turn our ship around and sail for home. I spend the journey thinking of Victor Frankenstein and his monster. It is an incredible tale—a tale that has now come to an end.